DAVID MORTIMORE BAXTER

Manners!

by Karen Tayleur

illustrated by Brann Garvey

Librarian Reviewer
Kathleen Baxter
Children's Literature Consultant
formerly with Anoka County Library, MN
BA College of Saint Catherine, St. Paul, MN
MA in Library Science, University of Minnesota

Reading Consultant
Elizabeth Stedem
Educator/Consultant, Colorado Springs, CO
MA in Elementary Education, University of Denver, CO

STONE ARCH BOOKS
Minneapolis   San Diego

First published in the United States in 2007
by Stone Arch Books, A Capstone Imprint
1710 Roe Crest Drive,
North Mankato, Minnesota 56003.
www.capstonepub.com

Published by arrangement with Black Dog Books.

Library of Congress Cataloging-in-Publication Data
Tayleur, Karen.
    Manners!: Staying Out of Trouble with David Mortimore Baxter / by Karen
Tayleur; illustrated by Brann Garvey.
    p. cm. — (David Mortimore Baxter)
    Summary: Young David Mortimore Baxter, who knows how to avoid making
embarrassing mistakes, shares his rules of etiquette pertaining to phone answering, car
travel, television watching, and nose picking.
    ISBN-13: 978-1-59889-075-4 (hardcover)
    ISBN-10: 1-59889-075-1 (hardcover)
    ISBN-13: 978-1-59889-207-9 (paperback)
    ISBN-10: 1-59889-207-X (paperback)
    [1. Etiquette—Fiction. 2. Humorous stories.] I. Garvey, Brann, ill. II. Title. III.
Title: Staying out of trouble with David Mortimore Baxter. IV. Series: Tayleur, Karen.
David Mortimore Baxter.
PZ7.T21149Man 2007
[Fic]—dc22   2006005075

Art Director: Heather Kindseth
Graphic Designer: Kay Fraser

Photo Credits
Delaney Photography, cover

Printed in China.
062017   010556R

Table of Contents

CHAPTER 1

MY WHO'S WHO

Ms. Stacey

Ms. Stacey is my teacher at school. She has very good manners. She is **always** trying to teach us good manners, but kids like **Jake Davern** make her job really hard.

Jake Davern (also known as **Monkey Boy**)

Jake Davern is a kid in my class. Sometimes he walks around like a chimpanzee, which is how he got the name Monkey Boy. Yes, I know chimpanzees are apes, not monkeys, but whatever.

Rose Thornton

Rose Thornton is the person I like the least in the whole world. Rose likes to think that she has good manners. But Rose can be really rude sometimes. She'd be very surprised to hear anyone say that, but it's **true**.

Victor Sneddon

Every school has one, and Victor Sneddon is ours. He is the **school bully**. If he has any manners, I haven't seen them yet. Victor is Rose Thornton's cousin. He REALLY likes my sister **Zoe**.

Joe Pagnopolous

Joe is my **best friend** and one of the members of **The Secret Club**. Joe likes watching movies and pretending to be characters from his favorite movies. He always says "please" and "thank you" at my house, so my mom thinks he's a nice boy.

Bec Trigg

Bec is my other **best friend** and the third member of The Secret Club. Bec has a **pet rat**, **Ralph**, who is also a member of our club. Bec is good at spitballs and art. She also has **good manners**.

Mr. McCafferty

Mr. McCafferty is my neighbor. He never misses a chance to call my parents and tell them that **I did something wrong**. Mr. McCafferty has a cat named **Mr. Figgins** who is just mean. I think Mr. McCafferty has some really *BAD* manners, like biting, but that's another story.

Mom

Mom is the *QUEEN* of manners. She has a very long list of good and bad manners. She doesn't let me get away with anything. She says she's *doing it for my own good*. I think she just likes **bossing me around.**

Dad

Dad likes the **big** good manners, like speaking **politely** and saying **please** and **thank you**. He doesn't know the huge list of manners that Mom knows. Sometimes he'll let you get away with bad manners **if no one is looking.**

Gran

Gran is so old that I think she actually **invented** some of the manners in this book. Gran's big thing is **table manners**. If you don't have 𝒢𝒪𝒪𝒟 table manners, then you'd better not eat at the same table as my gran. You would <u>never</u> hear the end of it.

Zoe

Zoe is my sister. She is older than me and thinks she's an adult. But she isn't. She's just a teenager who likes to **wear black** and talk on her **cell phone**. Zoe has some **good manners**, but sometimes she forgets them. Then she has bad manners. Usually *she uses her bad manners on me.*

Harry

Harry is my little brother. He has **no manners**. He knows about good manners, but he just ignores them. It's like Harry lives on **another planet**. Harry is really 𝔸ℕℕ𝕆𝕐𝕀ℕ𝔾.

Boris

Boris has no manners. He **slobbers** when he eats his food and farts whenever he wants to, even at the dinner table. Boris never says please or thank you. Sometimes he'll kick sand on you at the beach or make noise when you're trying to watch TV. Boris has the **worst manners** of the entire family. But I don't care. It's not his fault. Boris is my dog.

CHAPTER 2

WHAT ARE MANNERS?

There are many things that you are not supposed to do. When you do something like drive your **car too fast** or steal or **hurt someone**, it's called **breaking the law.** If you do something that's against the law, you will probably end up in JAIL. Then you won't get to do *anything fun anymore.*

But there's another group of laws. My mom calls them the "**unwritten laws.**" You could break these laws and you'd probably never end up in jail. But you might not have any friends. Gran is always pointing out my manners. One day, she said, "David, you just don't know the word etiquette."

She was right. I had to look it up in the **dictionary.**

etiquette (ET-uh-ket) n: Rules governing socially acceptable behavior.

I told Mom that etiquette and good manners sounded like the same thing. She said they pretty much were, but I looked up manners anyway.

manners (man-urz) n: The socially correct way of acting; etiquette.

I started thinking about the unwritten laws of good manners. Etiquette. I just didn't think it was fair. If these were rules we had to live by, why didn't someone just write them down?

So I did some **research** and **I wrote it all down.** It took me forever. I didn't know a lot about good manners, so I asked other people. Then I put it all together in this book.

This book will give you some idea of what to do, or what not to do, when it comes to **manners**.

You can read it from start to finish or from finish to start. (That's only easy to do if you can read backward.) You can pick your favorite number and go to that page. I don't really care how you do it. **Just do it**.

CHAPTER 3

NEIGHBORS

Balls/Frisbees

If your ball or frisbee goes into your neighbor's yard, it's good manners to ask your neighbor before you go into their yard to get it back. There's a good reason for this. If you just go in, **their dog might eat you**. Or they might have sprayed **poison** on their weeds and you might get it all over your hands.

Let's say one night you lose your ball. Then you go into the neighbor's backyard to get it. Let's call your neighbor Mr. McCafferty. Mr. McCafferty can't really see you because it's kind of dark. Then Mr. McCafferty thinks that a robber has come to steal all the good stuff from his house. (Even though I doubt he has any good stuff.)

Then Mr. McCafferty calls the **police** and the next thing you know there are sirens coming up the street. So you think that you should see what's going on.

Mr. McCafferty points at you and yells about a robber. The next thing you know, the police are shining their flashlights in your face. You look down at what you're holding. It's not the ball that you kicked so high and so far that it soared two backyards away. It is a round **garden gnome** with a beard. Mr. McCafferty **wants the police to arrest you**. And then you have a lot of explaining to do.

That's why you should always ask before you go in your neighbor's yard to find your ball.

Keep out

If you own a pet it should stay on your property. If you have a tiny white mouse, **you need to keep it in a cage.** It shouldn't go into someone else's home and scare them or eat all the cheese out of their refrigerator. I don't know how the mouse would open a refrigerator. If it did, it would probably go for the cheese. Unless it was sliced cheese wrapped in plastic. I **don't think** a little mouse could open the plastic. Also, I think mice like peanut butter better anyway. (**Ralph,** Bec's rat, will eat almost ANYTHING.)

If you have an elephant, you still have to keep it in your own backyard. Not only that, but you couldn't just let it stand in your backyard and let it reach over to the neighbor's apple tree or peanut tree or **marshmallow tree**. It would eat all the apples or peanuts or marshmallows.

It's against the real law to let your pet just wander around your neighbor's backyard. Especially if your dog is Boris and he leaves your neighbor a little present that your neighbor steps on and doesn't notice until he walks into his house.

If your neighbor wanted a MOUSE or an **elephant** or a dog, they would probably just get their own. So keep your pet to yourself.

Mail

Every now and then, our mail person delivers **someone else's envelope** to our mailbox. If you don't know the person whose name is on the envelope, you should take it back to the post office.

It could be a birthday card, or tickets to a Smashing Smorgan wrestling taping. Or something else special.

Once we got Mr. McCafferty's mail by mistake. I didn't read the envelope right. I thought it said Mr. D. Baxter, so I opened it. (The **handwriting** was really bad.)

When I realized the letter wasn't for me, I gave it to Mr. McCafferty. He went CRAZY. He yelled at me for reading his mail. I told him I don't read boring stuff like "Ten Tips for Healthy Roses." He asked how I knew that's what the letter was if I **hadn't read** it.

Then I said that I was only guessing that's what it was about because there was a picture of a flower on it. Mr. McCafferty called my mom. He said that he was sorry to call, but he needed to talk to her about me. Then I went home.

It's RUDE to open other **people's mail**. Imagine how you would feel if someone opened your mail. Unless it was a bill. Then maybe they would pay the bill for you. That would be GOOD.

Spying

Mom says it's bad manners to **spy** on your neighbors. So you shouldn't do it. But Joe and Bec and I play this game called Spies. The point of Spies is that you spy on people. Neighbors live close by, so it's really easy to spy on them. It's easier than having to go to another country or something.

Mom understands about the game. But she still says I shouldn't do it. She said that it makes Mr. McCafferty feel uncomfortable to have people spying on him while he's gardening. That's why, at the next **Secret Club** meeting, I'm going to vote for not spying on Mr. McCafferty while he's gardening. We'll just have to wait for him to do something else.

Window check

You shouldn't look through your **neighbor's windows** when there's no one home. Even if you think that your neighbor might be a murderer. Even if you think he might wrap his victims in the newspaper that he keeps in piles all around his house.

If you really think this, you should probably tell the police. They will need a search warrant to check it out. I know, because I've watched **TV shows** where police have had to do this. If the police don't get a search warrant, any evidence they find can't be used in court against the murderer. Then the judge says, "OVERRULED" a lot. Then the murderer is found not guilty and he'll probably come looking for you. Even if his name is Mr. McCafferty *and your mother says he's just a nice old man.*

You shouldn't even look in your neighbor's window when they are home. I did one afternoon. I saw something flashing in **Mr. M.'s** window. I thought he might be doing some experiments on bodies or something.

The next thing I knew, **Mr. McCafferty** tapped me on the shoulder. He asked me what I wanted. I had to make up a story about selling him some chocolates from school. Then he asked me where the chocolates were. I told him that the **chocolates melted** and that I would have to get some more from school. Then I went home and hoped he would forget about buying chocolates. **Just stay away.**

No littering

Chances are, if you drop your candy bar wrapper in your neighbor's gutter, the next time it rains it's just going to end up in **your** gutter. Then you'll have to pick it up. It's just easier to put the wrapper in your pocket and put in the garbage when you get home.

Be CAREFUL what you **put in your pocket**, though. Once I had a peach and put the peach pit in my jacket pocket. **Then I put my jacket in my locker**. That day, the weather got really hot. I left my jacket there.

Then, one day I was called to the principal's office. Mr. Woods, our principal, wanted to know **why there was a peach tree growing out of my locker**. I tried to explain about not littering and putting the peach pit in my jacket. He didn't get it. I had to clean out my whole locker. That was good, because I found a bunch of things that **had been missing**.

CHAPTER 4

TABLE MANNERS

Burping

Sometimes you don't even know a burp is coming until it suddenly **pops out**. If you do burp, you need to excuse yourself. "Pardon me," and "Oops, excuse me," are both okay. Saying "**Whoa, good one**," or "Wow, did you hear that?" or burping the national anthem is **not acceptable**. (Jake Davern can burp the entire alphabet without taking a breath. If you are going to try this, make sure there are no adults around.)

Eat, don't play

I saw this movie once where a man made a mountain out of his mashed potatoes. I've done this before. I made a mountain. Then I put three peas on top of the mountain and pushed them down. I pretended that the **peas were downhill skiers**. The first one down was the winner.

Harry and I were really getting into it. Even Dad was interested. But Mom said that the dining table *was no place for playing.*

Harry asked if we could leave the table to play with our food. He got **into trouble**.

The other thing Harry used to do was squeeze his food through his teeth. This works with mushy food, **especially when a tooth is missing.** Harry squeezed his food and it came out so fast that it knocked Gran's glass over. It was pretty COOL.

If you want to play with your food, make sure there are no adults around. **Don't get caught.** Harry spent a week cleaning out the pantry.

Knives

Once I saw a man lick his knife. He cut his tongue right off. It was AWFUL. It must have been a really sharp knife, because his tongue just slid along the knife. Then it fell off into his plate. People started screaming. Someone fainted. There was blood everywhere.

Okay, this **isn't true**. But it could happen. It's not only bad manners, it's plain common sense. **Just don't do it.**

Elbows on the table

For some reason, you're not supposed to rest your elbows on the dinner table. I think this comes from the time when people ate at the dining table with their **swords** at their sides. If they kept their elbows off the table it was **easier for them to pull their swords out for a quick fight** if someone interrupted their meal. (I'm not sure that this is true, but it sounds good.)

Eating with fingers

You're not supposed to eat with your fingers. You'll get your hands all **MESSY** and need to wipe them **somewhere**. You'll wipe them on your pants or shirt or the tablecloth. **It's easier to use utensils.**

Sometimes Mom lets us eat with our fingers. This is usually when we eat things like **pizza** or **hamburgers**. We definitely have to wash our hands right after we've finished. I let Boris lick my fingers once, but Mom said that was not sanitary. I guess she thought that I might give Boris germs or something.

Stuffing mouth

The thing about stuffing your mouth with food is that you need to breathe. You 𝕹𝔼𝓥𝔼ℝ know when someone is going to come along and hold your nose. Keeping space in your mouth means you can still breathe. Also, you could choke on all that food. **I don't want Harry giving me the kiss of life.**

Chewing with mouth open

At our school, you're not allowed to eat in class. If your teacher asks if you're chewing something and your mouth is **closed**, you can swallow it and say no.

This is okay, because you're not chewing something anymore. But if you chew with your mouth open, she'll be able to see you are chewing. Then you're in trouble. **Unless it's lunchtime.** Then it's okay for you to be eating.

Talking with mouth full

When I talk with my mouth full, my sister, **Zoe**, says, "*Say it, don't spray it!*" That's because tiny bits of food escape when you're talking. Also, people can't always **understand what you're saying**. I once told Mom, "**This is really good food.**" My mouth was full. She thought I said, "**Boris just made a poo.**" Poor Boris got into 𝕋ℝ𝕆𝕌𝔹𝕃𝔼.

Just Wait

It is good manners to wait until everyone at the table is served before you start to eat. Also, if we're having Mom's **veggie loaf** for dinner, I trade with Harry, because his piece is always smaller.

But if dinner is something I like to eat, I wait for the last helping. **It's usually the largest**.

Reaching for the salt

Don't ever reach over someone to get the salt. I only did it once. Mom invited Mr. McCafferty over for dinner and I **reached in front of him**. The next thing I knew, he bit down hard on my arm. He tried to tell everyone he was in the middle of taking a bite from *his corn*. But then he gave me a secret little smile. I think he was trying to **teach** me a lesson.

Picking your teeth

Mom hates it when someone picks their teeth at the table, even though we put **toothpicks** on the table every night. She thinks you should take the toothpick away from the table before you use it. If I have to use a toothpick, I just hide under the table. The last time I was down there, I saw Dad doing the same thing.

Using a napkin

In our family you get to choose what you want for dinner on your birthday. Mom likes going to **fancy restaurants**. As soon as you sit down, the waitress whips out a napkin and puts it in your lap. This is because they think you are really MESSY and will probably **drop some food on your clothes**.

You can use the napkin to clean your mouth, but once you've dropped it on the ground, you have to leave it there. That's because there are probably germs on the ground and you don't want to wipe them onto your mouth. You're NOT allowed to blow your nose with your napkin, either.

Gee, thanks

When you've eaten out, **always thank** the person who invited you. It DOESN'T matter if it was at a restaurant or at their house. Tell them **how nice it was, even if it wasn't**. Someone **took time** to prepare the food, or they paid for it. The least you can do is thank them.

You should **even thank** whoever does the cooking at your home. Don't get too carried away, though. **I thanked Mom for veggie loaf** one night and we've been having it once a week ever since.

Oops

If you drop something on the floor at a restaurant, you're supposed to **leave it there**. If it's a knife or fork, then the waiter will get you another one. If it's your food, you just have to leave it. (Even if it's fries.) At your home, it's probably okay to pick up stuff. At my house, we have a three-second rule. **Pick it up in three seconds** or less and you can eat it. I guess it takes three seconds for germs to jump on to food. They must only have little legs.

At our house, if you **drop food under the table,** it will disappear. Boris sits under there during dinner and he'll **eat anything**. I've lost a few napkins that way.

Nose blowing

My gran says it's RUDE to blow your nose at the table. This made things tricky **when I had a cold.** I sat there sniffing for five minutes. Then Mom went crazy and yelled at me for SNIFFING. I tried to wipe **my nose on my sleeve,** because that isn't blowing. But you're **not allowed** to do that either. You also can't use your brother's sleeve or the tablecloth or the napkin that you wipe your face with. Finally Gran told me that you **are supposed to leave the table and blow your nose somewhere else.** Feel free to do that, but don't get interested in what's on TV and forget to go back to the table. You'll get in trouble for that too!

Cell phones

I don't have a cell phone, but Zoe does. When we went to the Thorntons' house for dinner one night, Zoe was really annoyed. She asked Dad if she had to come. He said, **"Definitely."** Which means, **"You'd better come and I don't want to talk about it."**

So there we were, waiting for the dessert. Zoe pulled out her phone and started talking to some friend from school. It was way more interesting than the talk that was happening at the dinner table. Dad leaned over. Then he took her phone. He kept talking to Mr. Thornton like nothing had happened.

It was nice to see someone else get in TROUBLE for a change. Dad kept **Zoe**'s phone for a whole month.

Secret signal

When you're finished eating, you're supposed to put your knife and fork side by side on your plate. This tells people that you've finished eating. This does not work if you have a plate full of Mom's veggie loaf and you haven't eaten any.

This is COOL, because it's like a **secret signal**. Since I found out about this one, I've been thinking of other signals we could use in **The Secret Club**. Just be careful not to do it accidentally.

I did it once when we were at a restaurant and I left the table to blow my nose (see above). The thing is, I like to eat **my favorite food last**. There was a whole stack of french fries left on my plate. The waiter walked by, saw my secret signal, and took my plate away. **Mom wouldn't let me go into the kitchen to get it back.**

NO germ zone

Even when I took a shower the day before, Mom makes me **wash my hands** before we start to eat. She says I need to get rid of the germs on my hands. The thing is, Mom makes us use utensils (knives and forks and spoons) at the table. So, **the germs can not get on our food**. I tried telling her that, but she just made me wash my hands again.

Finger-licking good

If you get food on your fingers, **you're supposed to wipe them** on a napkin. If there is **no napkin,** you can't use your clothes, because you'll just get in trouble.

I'm lucky, because Boris sits under our dining table during meals. I can always wipe my hands on him.

The last piece

My dad says it's good manners to offer the last piece of something to someone else, before eating it up yourself. If you have to ask, **do it really, really quietly**. Really quietly. Don't even move your lips. Then when you get in trouble for taking the last piece of candy, **you can say that you asked**, but no one answered. Of course, probably no one will hear you, but at least you did the right thing. I always offer my **veggie loaf to Boris**, but Dad says that's not the same thing.

CHAPTER 5

EMBARRASSING MOMENTS

Excuse me . . .

It is embarrassing to see a friend with something in their teeth. Sometimes I'm not sure if their **teeth are green** or if it's just SPINACH.

How do you **tell them** without **making them embarrassed?** I've tried a few different things. I'll ask them if they **want a drink of water** and hope that that will wash the stuff away. I'll stick my lips out and lick my teeth and hope they copy me.

My little brother, Harry, just says things like, **"What's on your teeth?"** I would not recommend doing that. Sometimes you've just got to tell them.

Is that toilet paper?

If someone has **toilet paper** on their shoe, you should **point it out to them**. Chances are, they DIDN'T put it there on purpose.

(Unless they have used the "my foot was stuck in the toilet" excuse for being late to school.) I don't think you should be **embarrassed** to tell them. I mean, we all use the toilet. Everyone does. As my dad says, it's just a natural function.

The name game

I have a **brain** that just doesn't remember names. If you're like me, and you forget someone's name, the best thing to do is say, "I'm sorry, I can't remember your name."

This is okay if you've only met the person once before. When you've met them a couple of times, it gets trickier. (Especially if you need to introduce them to someone else.) You could say that you hit your head and can't remember anything. You could just mumble their name and hope they don't notice that you have no idea what their name is.

If they're at school, you could look at any books they're holding.

They should have their name on the book. You could **accidentally knock the books** out of their hands and check out the name when you help them pick the books up.

This doesn't always work. I once called a kid **Roget** because that was **the name on his book**. It turned out to be the name of the book, some kind of dictionary.

If none of these things work, faint. **I do that a lot.** It seems to work.

CHAPTER 6

BODY MANNERS

Better out than in

I think you know what I'm talking about.

Harry farted once in the living room. When Mom got mad, Harry said that it was **good manners in Zambodia**. Mom said that *we lived in Bays Park, not Zambodia*. Zoe said there was no such place as Zambodia. Mom said she didn't care if there was or not. She said that it was *bad manners and that Harry should stop*.

Dad just said, "**Listen to your mother**." But he had a little smile on his face.

We're not allowed to say the word "fart" in our house. Mom goes nuts if she hears it. We have to use other words instead. These are some of the words we use:

Dad: Better out than in.

Mom: Wind.

Zoe: Whoever dealt it, smelt it.

Harry: Who let Fluffy off the chain?

Joe: Who cut the cheese?

Bec: Who opened their lunch box?

Gran: (She doesn't say anything. She just pretends that farts don't exist.)

No matter what you call it, if you want to do it, do it in private. **Don't do it** on a **train** or **bus** or in the **school library**. Don't do it in a **crowded elevator** and pretend it was someone else. Don't even try it in an **empty elevator**. You'll just have to put up with it **all by yourself**.

That reminds me of the time we took **Boris** to the beach. He thought it was a pretty strange place. All that sand. All that water. He thought it was the **biggest water bowl** in the world. He tried drinking it all, but he stopped. It turns out that drinking sea water **does bad things to the insides** of dogs.

DOG

Boris farted the whole way home in the car.

It made **my eyes water**. It got **so bad** we had to stop the car and get out. The only one left inside the car was Boris. He looked pretty happy with himself. A **stinky, farting dog** is not only 𝔹𝔸𝔻 manners, it may also be dangerous for your health.

Pointing

I guess you're **not supposed to point at people**, because it's ℝ𝕌𝔻𝔼. I don't get that. Pointing is a lot easier than the conversation I had with Bec one day:

"See that guy over there," said Bec. "*He knows your sister, Zoe.*"

"**Which guy?**" I asked.

"The guy with the hair," said Bec.

"They all have hair," I said. "Just **point him out.**"

"I can't. It's *rude* to point."

"All right. **Describe him** then."

"The guy with the hair. *The blue hair*," said Bec. She was getting angry.

"There are four guys with blue hair," I said.

"The one second from the left," said Bec.

I POINTED to the guy she was talking about and she nodded. The guy looked at me and walked over.

"What are you **pointing at**?" he demanded.

Which is a good reason that you shouldn't point at someone.

Death breath

You cannot tell someone they have **bad breath**. You just can't. Unless they are a really close friend like Joe or Bec, and only if they **ask** if they have bad breath. Then you tell them YES. You don't say, "Bad? On a scale of one to ten you're a fifteen."

You can't tell other people at all. What you can do is **offer them a mint**. Even if you don't have a mint, offer them one. That way they should **get the idea** that their breath is **bad**. If they say they do want one and you don't have one, this could be a problem. Pretend you just dropped the last one on the floor.

Picky, picky

Sometimes there are things up your nose that just don't need to be there. You can **try blowing** your nose, but that doesn't always get these things out.

I think you know what I'm talking about. Boogies, boogers, snot. The worst is when your little brother catches you trying to dig one out and tells everyone, "David's picking his nose!" It's really **not good manners** to be found with your finger halfway up your nose. It's even worse when someone catches you flicking it.

It's not just **bad manners**. It can also be dangerous. There's a kid in our class named Jake Davern. One day he put his finger up his nose and he couldn't get it out again. Rose Thornton thought he was just faking it because we had a math test. Jake swore he really **couldn't get his finger out**. He had to go to the nurse and Mrs. Schtick, the school nurse, tried *everything to get it out*. She used ice and Vaseline and **even butter**. When she got out the toilet plunger Jake managed to pop his finger out.

If you really need to get something out of your nose, you should probably use a tissue.

Spit it out

You shouldn't be caught spitting. Sometimes I need to spit something out of my mouth. Then I have to go to the bathroom sink and spit it in there. Then **I wash it down the sink.**

The thing is, I could never make spitting look cool. Sometimes, the spit just dribbles down my chin and I **look like a baby**. Other times it ends up in places that I didn't aim for, like my shoes or, even worse, **Ms. Stacey's shoes.**

Victor Sneddon, our school bully, thinks it is very cool to spit. He used to do it all the time. But one day **he tried to spit out of the school bus window.** The wind caught his spit. It flew straight back into his face. Everybody laughed. Victor got in trouble and had to sit at the front of the bus.

Gran says that only camels can get away with SPITTING in public. And they're animals, so they don't count. They're also not known for their **good manners**.

CHAPTER 7

BEING POLITE

Sharing

Sharing is a **really hard thing to do**. Let's face it: It's not normal for a human being to have to share their stuff with other people. You want to keep it all to yourself. Unless it's something you don't really like (for example, veggie loaf). That is a good time to share things.

In the olden days, when we were cave people, the only way you could bring home a roast was to get the other guys to help you. **Woolly mammoths** were like two hundred feet tall or something. So you and some other guys killed the mammoth. Then you put it in the shopping cart and took it home. You had to share it because you all killed it together. Also, you didn't have a refrigerator, so the meat didn't stay fresh very long. Maybe that's where sharing started.

Also, back then, I think that you had to wipe your feet on the "Cave Sweet Cave" mat before you went inside. I'm pretty sure **mothers** were saying, "Wipe your feet. I just washed this floor." Some things NEVER change.

The good thing about sharing is that someone might share something with you. Sometimes Joe shares his lunch with me when his mom makes a cake. Mrs. P. makes the **best cakes**. She always gives enough to Joe to share with Bec and me.

Cover your nose

When you sneeze, there's a really good chance that something might come out of your nose. Even if you don't have a cold. And if you happen to be talking to someone and something comes out of your nose, then the something that comes out will end up on the person you are talking to. You might think it's really funny that they are now wearing what was once hanging around inside your nose. But they probably won't think it is.

When you explain that it was an accident, they will probably chase you around the schoolyard until you promise to take home their shirt and wash it. And Victor – I mean, they – still won't forgive you. Also, if you cough or sneeze on someone, you're just spreading your germs around. **They're your germs. Keep them to yourself.**

Just listen

Listening is hard. Sometimes, while someone is talking to me, I think of something really good. If I don't say what my good idea is, it disappears. You could carry a notepad around with you and **write down your idea** while the person is talking to you. I don't know if this is bad manners or not. I think it's okay. The reason you shouldn't talk while someone else is talking is that you might miss out on something. Like, "**Who wants chocolate?**" or "**Do you want to go to the movies?**"

Greeting people

The word "**hello**" is only five letters long. How hard can it be to say? Say it loud enough so people can hear you.

My dad shakes hands with people he meets. Sometimes he'll kiss ladies on the cheek. I think **kissing** is going **too far**. The thing about shaking hands is, it's really tricky to know when to do it. I've watched Dad. There doesn't seem to be any kind of rule about it. If I decide to shake someone's hand, I'll stick my hand out. Sometimes they're looking the other way and don't see it. If I think they're not going to shake my hand, I'll quickly zip my hand up to my head, like I was just fixing my hair or something. There's nothing more embarrassing than having your hand sticking out there, **like a limp fish gasping for air.**

My **Uncle Michael** always makes me shake hands when we see each other.

He grabs my hand and SQUEEZES it. Then he pumps it up and down. Like he's expecting **water to come out of my mouth or something.**

You can stick to saying hello clearly.

The magic words

I don't know if you've noticed this, but it's like some words are magical.

When you say "**please**" to people, sometimes they do something for you or give you stuff that they never meant to give you.

Be careful how you say it, though. Harry takes the word please and makes it into "**pleeeeeeeeeze**." **That is just annoying.** Don't do it.

Also, "thanks" is okay, but "thanks, Mom" or "thank you" is even better. It makes people want to help you if you ever ask for anything.

Shut your mouth

Shutting your mouth is a good idea because you don't know what might get into your mouth. I know an old lady who **swallowed a fly** because she yawned without covering her mouth. Then she swallowed a **spider** to catch the **fly**. Then she swallowed a **bird** to catch the spider. Then she swallowed a **cat** to catch the bird . . . ummm, hang on. I think that was a nursery rhyme.

Anyway, close your mouth, because you might swallow something you don't want to. Also, **no one wants to see what you had for breakfast.**

Cap back on

Mom says that it's good manners to put the cap back on the TOOTHPASTE. I don't think it's a big deal. Sometimes I leave the **cap off** because I think Harry's going to brush his teeth soon. But he doesn't and the **paste dries out.** Or the cap escapes onto the top of the bathroom cabinet.

Once I left the cap off and accidentally **leaned on the toothpaste tube**. I was trying to change Mom's mirror from the normal side to that side where everything looks **really huge**. Anyway, I leaned on the tube and the paste just squirted EVERYWHERE. It was fun, but then Mom went crazy and **I had to clean up the whole bathroom**.

Just put the cap **back on**.

CHAPTER 8

Seat up, seat down

Mom says that it's **really bad manners** to leave the seat up after I use the bathroom. I didn't see what the big deal was. Then I found out.

One day, Mom told me about the time she was living in the country and her family had this toilet in the yard. **It wasn't a flush toilet or anything modern.** It was an **OUTHOUSE**. It was a can with a toilet seat on it. One night my mom went to the bathroom, way down the path, right to the bottom of the garden. Mom sat down in the dark. Someone had left the seat up, and Mom fell in the can. Right up to her armpits. **She was there for hours yelling before someone came to rescue her.** They had to hose **her off** outside. Mom **laughs** whenever she tells this story, but I don't see anything funny about it.

I make sure **I put the seat down now.**

No-go zone

When I was little, I used to open the toilet door when Mom or Dad was using the bathroom. I'd stand there and talk to them. Sometimes I'd even bring my friends in so they could **join in the conversation.** Mom and Dad would get really upset. They said that the bathroom was one place where they needed their **PRIVACY.** That's when I found out it was bad manners to **invade someone's privacy.** So now the only thing I say to someone who's using the bathroom is "**Are you almost done?**"

I definitely **don't** open the door.

On a roll

At my house, no one wants to change the toilet roll when the old one's finished. We have a whole basket of toilet paper near the toilet. Everyone leaves **one sheet of toilet paper** on the roll that's in the holder, and **uses the toilet paper from the basket.** Then finally, Mom will **flip out** and say, "*Am I the only one who changes the toilet roll?*" And then she'll change it.

The answer to her question is **YES**. I don't know why she asks, because she already knows the answer. I think holders for toilet paper are overrated.

To read or not to read?

I think it's okay to **read a boring book** in the bathroom. Junk mail is even better. Then this won't happen: You won't get too into reading something and forget to get off the toilet. You won't make everyone wait outside for the next hour, banging on the door, while you say, "**Just a minute, just a minute.**" And Mom won't have to come and yell, "**Do I have to break down this door?**" before you get out. (**Yeah, Dad.**)

CHAPTER 9

TV

Remote hog

When Dad is home, he is the **official** remote control 𝓗𝓞𝓖𝓖𝓔𝓡. He only finds the channels that have news or sports or documentaries. You can't just wait for Dad to fall asleep in his chair. He might be snoring loudly and you might use all your **spy skills to get the remote**, but before you change the channel, he'll say, "**I'm watching that.**" Yeah, right, Dad.

Too loud

TV too loud? That's just 𝓑𝓐𝓓 manners.

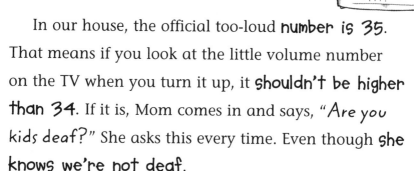

In our house, the official too-loud **number is 35.** That means if you look at the little volume number on the TV when you turn it up, it **shouldn't be higher than 34.** If it is, Mom comes in and says, "Are you kids deaf?" She asks this every time. Even though **she knows we're not deaf.**

The problem is, some shows are quiet, so we turn the TV up. But when the commercials come on, **they're really loud.** Zoe said she is going to do a paper on it when she gets to college.

Something I have noticed is that you can turn up the TV a couple of notches at a time and no one notices. I did this **one day as an experiment.** It took me twenty minutes but I got the volume up to **42.** Dad didn't even notice. Then an ad came on. Mom came in and yelled, *"Are you kids deaf?"*

Then Dad said, *"What?"* and Harry and I cracked up.

When I have my own house, I'll know when the TV is too loud, because the floor will vibrate.

Sssshhhhhh

There is nothing worse than watching a show and trying to figure out who did what and then right at the end your brother comes in and starts talking to you about his newest baseball card. Or he tells you that Boris left something on the front porch that's really strange-looking and in the shape of a pyramid.

It's NOT fair. You never do find out **who the bad person was.** Just when you start yelling at your brother for interrupting your show, he settles onto the couch and tells you to be quiet because his show is on. Then you start shouting **because you're mad.** Then your mom comes in and tells you to be quiet because your brother is watching his favorite show.

Sorry about that. I got a little carried away. What I mean is it's rude to speak when someone is watching a show. Wait for the commercials before you talk to them. (Unless it's an emergency like **your kitchen's on fire.**)

CHAPTER 10

PHONE

Greetings

When you answer the phone, you should be polite. Say something like, "Hello, it's David. May I ask who's calling?" Don't say it's David if your name isn't David. Use your own name.

You shouldn't do or say these things:

1. "Yeah? What?"

2. "City morgue, Zombie speaking."

3. Leave the phone to find your sister, then get distracted by something on TV or start playing with your dog.

Eavesdropping

The thing about listening in on other people's conversations on the phone is that you only get one half of the conversation.

If you only hear half of the conversation, sometimes you might get the **wrong idea** about what is going on. Like the other day. This was Zoe's half of a phone conversation:

"Oh hi. Did you see it?"

Pause.

"I know. Totally. What was she thinking?"

Pause.

"I know. What color was that? Swamp green? It was definitely from another planet."

That's when I really got interested.

"I know. You're right. She's lucky she didn't end up in jail."

Did someone help an alien? I thought.

"Did you check the feet?"

The alien must have had weird feet. Or lots of them. I wondered if I should tell Dad.

"Absolutely. I know what you're saying. If she brings that green thing along again, I'm out of there."

That's when I ran and told Dad that Zoe was hanging out with someone who was helping a green alien. Dad thought that probably wasn't true, but then I told him about the phone call.

When Zoe got off the phone, Dad asked her about the alien. Then it got confusing, because Zoe didn't know anything about an alien. So I repeated her phone conversation. It turned out she'd been talking about someone's new boyfriend.

It just goes to show how wrong you can be if you listen to another person's phone conversation.

If you have two phones in your house, you can always pick up the other phone to listen. The problem is, there's a **click** when you do that. Then your teenage sister comes and finds you. She rips the phone away and calls you SNEAKY and says that she's going to tell Mom.

That's what happens in our house, anyway.

Phone hog

If you are the only person who lives in your house, then it's okay for you to hog the phone. In my house there are five people. Each person has at least **five friends** that they need to talk to at some time. That could mean up to twenty-five calls in one day.

Zoe is the **phone hog** in our family. We have a cordless phone, which is sometimes a good idea but sometimes isn't. The good thing is that you can take the phone into a room where no one else can listen to your conversation. The bad thing is that Zoe can take the phone and we never see it again **until it is time for it to be recharged.**

One night, my gran was convinced that everyone in our house was dead. She thought that a murderer had killed us and then **taken the phone off the hook.** (Okay, this is a strange idea, but my **gran is strange.**) So she sent the police to check our house. What they found was one teenage girl hogging the phone.

Another time I missed out on some information because Joe couldn't get through on the phone. Okay, the information wasn't that important, but it could have been!

So you need to share the phone. **If you have a teenager in the house**, you might want to draw a chart.

Dinner calls

I know that it's bad manners to answer a phone call at dinner. Sometimes you just have to.

If I know that Mom's making a **new recipe**, I get Joe to call me around dinnertime. I just tell Mom that it's about homework. Then I try to stay on the phone until everyone **has finished eating**. I think Mom might be onto me. Last time I tried it, she brought my dinner to me in my room. Then she stood there while I ate it. I had to make up all this fake homework stuff to Joe who did not get it.

"So I think if you multiply that number by nine, you'll get your answer," I said to Joe, shoving some green and red stuff into my mouth.

"What?" said Joe.

"You're right," I said.

Mom still hadn't left. "This is really great," I told her.

"That's good," said Mom, but she still didn't leave.

"So, about that problem, Joe," I said.

"What?" said Joe.

It went on like that until I finished my dinner. Then Mom left. Maybe I won't try that anymore.

Late calls

My mom has this weird thing about the phone ringing after 9:30 at night. If it rings later than that, she thinks something is wrong, like a tragedy has happened. Also, she hates it when people call and everyone at our house is in bed.

Only call someone late at night when it's really **IMPORTANT**. Like, "**Can you tell me who the new player is for the football team?**" or "So, what is your favorite color?" or something like that.

Get the message

When you take phone messages, you need to get all the information. Then you should write it down so you don't forget it. Then don't lose the scrap of paper you wrote it down on.

You can't just say, "**Oh yeah, someone called for you yesterday, Mom. He said something about urgent and red and a horse.**" Mom gets cranky when I do things like that. That's why we have a pad near our phone to write down the messages.

The last time I forgot a phone message, Mom and Dad ended up at a party dressed as **Tweedledum** and **Tweedledee**. I'm not sure who was who. The message was for them to come in **normal clothes**, because the costume part of the party **had been cancelled**.

MOM and DAD
COSTUME
PARTY at
8:00PM is
CANKELED

I don't know what they were so mad about. I thought they looked fine.

Tell, don't yell

My brother Harry has a really annoying habit. When he answers the phone, he **yells out** who the call is for. He does it without taking the phone away from his mouth. By the time someone else answers the phone, the person on the other end is deaf. **It is just plain bad manners to make someone deaf**. So don't do it.

Too much information

You should never say, "Sorry, my dad can't come to the phone right now because **he's on the toilet.**" **(Especially if that's true.)** Or, "Zoe says she hates talking to you." Or "Mom said if it's a telemarketer, I don't want to talk to them." Just tell the caller that the person they want to talk to can't come to the phone. **Ask them to call back**. Then don't answer the phone the next time it rings.

CHAPTER 11

THE MOVIE THEATER

Big hair

If you have really big hair or a special wig or hat on for your trip to the movies, it's polite to stay out of other people's way. There's nothing worse than not being able to see the middle of the screen because of someone's head.

If you are a really tall person, don't sit in front of a short person, like me. It just means that I am going to sit on my backpack. Then the person behind me won't be able to see.

Once, I was watching a really scary movie. There was a **lady with big hair sitting in front of me.** The theater was PACKED. I couldn't move. I tried coughing to get her attention, but Joe just shoved his drink at me. Finally I leaned forward, parted the big hair right down the middle and peeked through. **I did it gently, so the lady didn't know.**

Then, at a really scary spot, she jumped in fright. I was left holding her hair. It was a **wig**. She didn't notice I had it, so I put it back on her head and sat down in my seat. At the end of the movie, I realized I'd put it back on the man next to her. The lady looked at him and screamed. Joe and I got out of there really quickly.

Rustling snacks

Most of the movies I see are really NOISY. Sometimes, though, there will be a really quiet part of the movie. Usually just before something really loud happens. If you have a bag of chips or a noisy plastic bag of candy, wait until the noise on the screen gets louder before you open it and make a lot of noise rustling the package around. Otherwise, other people might miss out on some really important information. Also, they might want to have some of your chips and then you'll have to share.

So I said . . .

What I can't understand is anyone who would pay for movie tickets, sit down in the theater, then **talk for the whole movie**. Not only is it **bad manners**, it just **doesn't make sense**. Save your money and sit in a park and talk. Or, pay me money to come and sit in my room with the light out. If you need to talk in the dark, **go to outer space** and talk there.

And then . . .

There is nothing more annoying than going to a movie with someone who **tells you what is going to happen next** all the way through the movie. My friend Joe is like that. If Joe really likes a movie, he will see it five or six or even more times. By the sixth time, he can repeat the best parts **word for word**. If I wanted him to do that, I'd just stay at home and let Joe repeat the movie for me. **I would rather watch a movie** and not know what's going to happen. So would the people behind me. That's why I always buy Joe an extra large **bucket of popcorn to help keep him quiet**.

Turn around

When you go to the movie theater, the seats all face in the same direction. They face in the direction of the screen. This is because you sit on your seat and watch the screen. **That's what normal people do.** Sometimes, though, there are people (*usually little kids*) who turn around during the movie to look at you. Then they might **sing a little song** that has got nothing to do with the movie. Then they might **bob up and down**. When you ask them to turn around, they just ignore you and maybe kick out at you and **tip over your extra large bucket** of popcorn that you've just spent all your money on to keep Joe quiet. This is bad manners and should not be encouraged. **The best thing you can do is probably move.**

Phone off

Hearing a phone **RING** during a **pirate movie** just ruins the whole thing. Answering your phone is even **ruder than leaving your phone on.**

Unless the film is terrible, keep your phone **off**. If it's boring, at least talk loud enough so that everyone can listen in.

Feet down

You shouldn't put your feet on the seat at the movies. This is because you don't always know what you've been walking in. You might **step in something that Boris didn't mean to leave** in the laundry and then put your feet on the seats and then the next person to sit on the seat is sitting in Boris' present. The only thing worse than that is **if that person is you.**

CHAPTER 12

No drooling

The thing about traveling in our car is that the back seat is always full. Unless someone stays home, of course. It's even worse if Boris comes along for the ride. (But that's another story.)

We are supposed to have this system where everyone in the back seat gets a turn to be in the middle. It's a great idea, but it never happens. Zoe, who can be really slow at other things, is always the **first into the car**, in a window seat. She'll have her headphones on and her eyes closed and totally ignore you when you tell her to move to the middle. You do not want to get Zoe mad. Even **Victor Sneddon** is scared of her.

Harry is just a whiner. If he has to sit in the middle, he **moans** and **groans** and leans forward and **pokes** Mom and Dad. Then Mom makes me switch places with him.

So there I am, in the **middle seat**.

Everyone knows the window seats are the best because you get to rest on the window and go to sleep. But the middle person (me) has to do the head snap. That's when you close your eyes, **doze off**, and feel your head tipping left or right. Then you snap awake and start all over again.

Sometimes, though, you finally fall asleep on the person next to you. Then you get **poked in the ribs** to wake up and get off them. This is your chance to say you've never been asleep. That's when you notice a patch of your sleep drool on their shoulder. Getting **sleep drool** on someone else is very bad manners. You should always apologize and try to mop it up. The best way to prevent **sleep drool** is:

a) stay awake

b) get a window seat

c) stuff your mouth with a sponge before you fall asleep.

Rude Faces

Making **rude faces** through the window of
the car or bus you are traveling in is very **bad
manners**. It may frighten the person you are making
faces at. It may also get you into **very big trouble**.

Once my whole school went camping at the beach.
It was a really long bus trip and Jake Davern, also
known as **Monkey Boy**, got bored. So he decided
to try some of his **monkey faces** on the passing
drivers. Jake is known for his bad ideas. That was
another one.

When we got to the beach, a car pulled up behind
our bus. It was the same car Jake had been making
faces at. It looked just like the car that our principal,
Mr. Woods, drove. That's because it was his car. Jake
Davern had to miss out on the first campfire night
and wash and dry the dishes for the entire school.

Oh, and one other thing. My mom used to say
that **if I made a face, I might stay like that.** I
never believed her until I met Jake Davern.

I've never made a face since. Jake looks like a monkey, whether he's making a face or not.

Waiting

When we go on trips for school, sometimes the bus stops for a **bathroom break**. This is a good time to get off and stretch your legs. Sometimes we stop where there are souvenirs and people buy something. Bathroom breaks are not long stops.

When we went on our gold-mining trip, we stopped at this great place called "**Gold Rush.**" It had lots of toilets and lots of food and fun things to buy. Ms. Stacey told us we had to be back on the bus in fifteen minutes. Forty minutes later, we were still waiting for my friend Joe to get back on the bus. Joe couldn't decide between the rugged, fake leather hat or the genuine plastic gold pan. In the end he bought the small, plastic tube with the flake of something gold in it. By the time he got back on the bus, everybody was ready to yell at him, **gold or no gold**.

When you are traveling with other people, it is **good manners to think about them,** not just yourself. Otherwise you might be cleaning up the bus while everyone else is having dinner.

Keep it clean

When you are traveling with others, especially if you're sharing a room or a tent, **it is probably a good idea to take a shower every now and then.** It is very bad manners to camp for one week in a small tent with your friend and not change your shoes or socks or underwear and not take a shower. Especially in the hot weather. Unless your friend is Joe and he has not changed his shoes or socks or underwear either and hasn't even thought of taking a shower.

When Ms. **Stacey** inspected our tent at the end of our camping week, **she actually passed OUT.** Luckily, Joe is very quick sometimes. He grabbed the sock off his left foot and waved it under Ms. Stacey's nose. He said later he'd got the idea from the smelling salts that are used to wake up wrestlers.

It worked really well. Ms. Stacey woke up, grabbed the sock from Joe, and threw it into the bushes. Then she lectured us both and we missed out on a last chance at the **Flying Fox ride**. Then Joe got in trouble at home because he'd lost one of his socks.

I keep wondering what wild animal ended up with Joe's sock. Hopefully the sock didn't kill anything.

CHAPTER 13

ON THE BEACH

Towel trouble

People go to the beach to get some **rest**. They're usually looking for a little time alone. That's why it's really bad manners to **put your towel** right next to someone at the beach, especially if you don't know them. There's nothing scarier than **opening your eyes to find a complete stranger one inch away from you.**

If this happens, it is okay for you to ask them to move over a little. But do it POLITELY.

Sand ban

Kicking sand is only fun when you are the person kicking it. It just gets in people's eyes, clothes, food, and their drinks, and it makes them **really crabby.**

Then they might get mad and pick you up and take you to the water and throw you in, even if you can't swim. And then you might **drown or a shark** might eat you and then everyone would be sad **(unless Rose Thornton was thrown in)** and that would ruin a good day at the beach. So **don't do it**.

Shake it all about

When dogs get out of the water after swimming or taking a bath, the first thing they do is shake their bodies. That's because **DOGS** haven't learned how to **use a towel to dry off**. Humans, though, know all about towels. When you come out of the water, it is not polite to shake the water off you all over the nearest person. Especially if that nearest person is warm and dry and wants to stay that way. If the nearest person wanted to get wet, they would go for a swim. People who shake water onto other people **think they are very funny**. But they aren't funny. In fact, **they're just being rude**.

Castles

One of the things sand is really good for is making sandcastles. There are a few good manners and rules that you need to know about **making castles:**

1. Dry Sand

Sometimes the sand is **too dry**. You need to get it wet to make it stick. If you are making the castle with someone else, you need to go all the way down to the water, fill the bucket, and bring it back to the castle. If you have a younger **brother** or **sister**, they might just like to do this all the time, because they like to run. Otherwise, you should take turns running for the water.

2. Sabotage

If you are making a sandcastle and the person next to you is making a sandcastle that is much better than yours, you shouldn't make their castle **collapse**.

Even if you say, "Hey, I've got a really good idea," and you show them how to make a tunnel in their castle but you make it so big that their tunnel collapses. Then they cry and tell their mom, who just happens to be your mom too, and then you get **into lots of trouble**.

3. Jumping

The **best thing** about making sandcastles is jumping on them.

Some people don't agree with me. If you want to jump on a sandcastle, you should make your own. Then you **can jump on it and everyone is happy**.

If you want to jump on a sandcastle and someone else made it, you **should ask first**. They might let you jump on it. Or they might want to jump on it themselves. Or they might just want to leave it as a sandcastle.

Anyone who has ever made a sandcastle (and I've made plenty of them) knows that the waves are just going to come and **smash it all over anyway**. So what's the big deal?

Beach litter

Sometimes there won't be a can to put your **garbage** in at the beach, so bring a plastic bag so you can take your trash home with you.

Littering is **against the real law**, but it's also just **bad manners**. Leaving trash in the sand is like making a **waste dump treasure hunt**. Imagine digging sand to make a castle and finding a **mushy sandwich**. Some things left in the sand can be really dangerous. Glass, or even **sharp plastic**, can cut someone's foot if they stand on it. Also, stuff like plastic bags **can hurt or kill wildlife**.

I just think it's a dumb thing to do. As Ms. Stacey says, "You wouldn't litter in your bedroom." But then again, she hasn't seen **my room**.

CHAPTER 14

That's about it.

I showed this book to Gran. She thinks that if I followed all the good manners in this book, I'd be able to have **dinner with the President**. I'd rather have dinner with Smashing Smorgan, but I didn't say that. You know why? Because it was good manners not to.

Mom said it was a good book but **she wanted me to take out the word "fart."** Dad said I should have put it in alphabetical order, but that sounded like too much work. I haven't shown Zoe or Harry yet. They could learn a lot just by reading a couple of pages.

When I read over all the rules about good manners one thing stands out. If it hurts someone else, then it's probably bad manners. If I knew that before, I wouldn't have had to spend all my time writing this book.

Wait. Where are my manners? There's something else I have to tell you. **This is the end**.

About the Author

When Karen Tayleur was growing up, her father told her many stories about his own childhood. These stories continued to grow. She says, "I always enjoyed the retelling, and wanted to create a character who had the same abilities with 'bending the truth.'" And David Mortimore Baxter was born! Karen lives in Australia with her husband, two children, two cats, and one dog.

About the Illustrator

Brann Garvey grew up in the great state of Iowa, where he studied art and visual communications. He graduated from the Minneapolis College of Art and Design with a degree in illustration. Brann is usually found with one or more of the following: a pencil in his hand, a comic book, a remote for watching DVDs, or his pet kitty, Iggy. When the weather is nice, Brann likes to play disc golf, and he proudly points out that Iowa is one of the world's centers for the sport. Iggy does not play.

Glossary

deaf (DEF)—not being able to hear well or to hear at all

eavesdropping (EEVZ-drop-ing)—listening secretly to the private conversation of others

etiquette (ET-uh-ket)—rules that tell you how to behave; how to act properly

gnome (NOME)—in legends and fables, a small human-like creature that lives underground

hygienic (hye-JEN-ik)—clean and healthy

littering (LIT-ur-ing)—leaving trash around

manners (MAN-urz)—good behavior

morgue (MORG)—a place where dead bodies are kept and examined

pantry (PAN-tree)—a kitchen closet

polite (puh-LITE)—showing good manners

sabotage (SAB-uh-tazh)—destroying someone's property on purpose

telemarketer (tel-uh-MAR-kuh-tur)—someone who uses the telephone to sell goods or services

vital (VYE-tuhl)—very important

Discussion Questions

1. Which manners in this book do you agree with? Which do you disagree with? Why?

2. Has David Mortimore Baxter forgotten to list any manners? What would you add to this book? Explain why.

3. On page 20, David is not sure why it isn't polite to put your elbows on the table while eating. What do you think the reason is for this rule?

4. On pages 74 and 75, read the section about "Sabotage." What does it mean to sabotage someone? Talk about other examples of sabotage that you have seen or been a part of.

Writing Prompts

1. How do you define "manners"? What manners are insisted upon at your house? Write also about how you feel about these expectations. Do you agree with them or not?

2. Write a list of table manners for eating at school. Explain each one. (Try David Mortimore Baxter's humorous style of writing).

3. Every family has different ways of eating dinner together. They have different table manners, too. Write and describe how your family eats a meal together, from start to finish.

David Mortimore Baxter

David is a great kid, but he has one big problem — he can't stop talking. These wildly humorous stories, told by David himself, will show readers just how much trouble a boy and his mouth can get into, whether he's making promises to become class president or bragging that he's best friends with the world's most famous wrestler. David is amiable, engaging, cool, and smart enough to realize that growing up is the biggest adventure of all.